King Snake

King Snake

Original title: Biography of a King Snake

by BURKE DAVIS

Illustrated by Albert Michini

SCHOLASTIC BOOK SERVICES

NEW YORK · TORONTO · LONDON · AUCKLAND · SYDNEY

For Chuck

Text copyright © 1975 by Burke Davis. Illustrations copyright © 1975 by Albert Michini. This edition is published by Scholastic Book Services, a division of Scholastic Magazines, Inc., by arrangement with G. P. Putnam's Sons, publishers of the book under the title BIOGRAPHY OF A KING SNAKE.

12 11 10 9 8 7 6 5 4 3 2 1   9   6 7 8 9/7 0 1/8

Printed in the U.S.A.   02

On a warm day in early June, deep inside a crumbly rotten log in the woods, a dozen small white eggs began to move. Weeks before, in early spring, a mother king snake had laid her eggs here in a forest in northern Virginia and crawled away, leaving her young to hatch and grow on their own.

Now a tiny sharp bone, no larger than the point of a pin, broke through one of the shells. This tiny bone was the egg tooth. Its only use was to break out of the egg, and after two or three days it would fall off.

Again and again, the tiny snake pecked and cut at the shell until, after about an hour, the head of the first baby snake pushed out. A second shell was soon broken, and then a third.

For two days the young snakes twisted and turned until the last of them was free of its soft shell. Then the young snakes began to crawl from the log into the sunlight. The slender snakes were already ten or eleven inches long, with bright-yellow bands across their black skins.

These were eastern king snakes, of a kind that lives from Delaware and Maryland south to Florida, and from the Atlantic to the Allegheny Mountains. Eight other kinds of king snakes, of slightly different colors, live throughout most of the United States except for the very northern and northwestern states. Still more kinds of king snakes are found in other countries.

The largest of the young snakes slid through the leaves and began hunting for food. He was hungry. A spider moved. The snake struck swiftly, took the spider in his jaws, and swallowed it. Soon afterward, as he nosed under a piece of bark, out crawled a centipede, with many legs. The young snake ate the centipede. Because of his long body, the king snake was able to digest large meals, and he ate as many insects as he could find.

When the baby snakes grew too warm in the sun, they burrowed under a cool tree trunk. They were "cold-blooded" reptiles, so that the heat of their bodies changed with the temperature about them. They would die if they became too hot.

Within a few days the snakes began to shed their skins. As the old skins dried and grew larger, they expanded, at first in loose wrinkles and then in sheets that peeled from the young snakes as they crawled. They were blind for a few hours as the skin loosened and came off, for they also shed the skin over their eyeballs. Like all snakes, they had no eyelids and were unable to blink their eyes.

During the shedding the young snakes raised their heads and flickered their forked tongues from their mouths more often than ever, for the long tongues drew chemicals from the air so that the snakes could "smell" other creatures and identify those they ate for food or others that might be dangerous. They could hear, but not with ears the way people hear. Snakes have no

ear openings in the head; they hear sounds through vibrations in the inner ear, where tiny delicate bones tap together lightly when noises are made nearby—almost like the ringing of a small hammer on an anvil.

Soon all the skins were shed, and the new black and yellow scales of the young king snakes gleamed in the Virginia sunshine. For the rest of their lives the snakes would shed each summer.

Within a few weeks the young snakes had gone in different directions and were living apart in the woods and fields. Each one hunted its own food and found its own burrow for sleeping or for shelter from the hot sun. They grew rapidly, and their skins stretched as they grew.

The largest of the young king snakes, the first-born, was now more than a foot and a half long. He explored the edge of the forest where he had been born and sometimes crawled into a nearby meadow or along the banks of a stream. He ate grasshoppers, beetles and roaches, and turtle eggs that he dug from the damp soil with his sharp head, and sometimes he drank from the edge of the stream.

One morning the young king snake met a brown snake whose body was almost as long as his own, but was not so thick and strong. The king snake struck at once; but since king snakes are not poisonous, his bite was harmless, and he had to squeeze his prey to death. He wrapped himself about the brown body, around and around, squeezing until his victim no longer moved. The king snake then began to eat the brown snake. It was a long time before he could swallow the body. His jaws opened wide upon hinges until his head seemed about to split, and the brown snake began to disappear. A large lump moved down the king snake. For two or three days the young king snake slept with a swollen body, until he had digested his meal.

Until the end of summer the young snake roamed his small territory, looking into every hole and cranny he could find. When large animals passed, making loud noises, the king snake hid in the grass or lay still among the leaves. Sometimes he swam the stream, and some days he lay in the sun or burrowed in the earth beneath old logs. Autumn had come. As the weather became colder, he did not grow so much as before. He was not as hungry as he had been at birth. At last he grew no longer. He crawled more slowly and spent more time sleeping in the warm sun.

One chilly day he crawled under a log, deeper than he had been before, burrowing until he could curl up under the earth and rotten wood. There he would sleep through the winter, while snow and ice piled high, far above him. Like many other living things in the woods and fields, he was hibernating.

For months the young king snake lay still, hardly moving or breathing. His heart beat slowly, and he did not need to find food or water to keep himself alive. His body had stored fat during the summer and used that for food while he slept.

The young snake did not come out of his burrow and up into the light again until March, when the air was warm once more. He was much thinner than he had been in the autumn, and for a time he hunted day and night, until he was no longer hungry. Within a week or two his body was plump again, and he had begun to grow once more.

In his second summer the young snake became a fine hunter. He ate many insects and sometimes stalked mice and lizards, which he caught with swift strokes. He found buried turtle eggs and once ate four birds' eggs from a nest he found high in the meadow grasses. He coiled about the grass stalks and swallowed the eggs, one by one, while a male and female redwing blackbird fluttered around him, shrieking.

When the snake had gone, the blackbirds looked
for a new tuft of grasses and began another nest.

The king snake crawled through the marsh, sunned himself for a few minutes on the bank of a narrow stream, and glided into the water, swimming with long, easy motions of his black and yellow body. Only his head was held above the water. A shadow swept across the stream and vanished. The snake swam on, unaware of the danger overhead.

Through the air, now sailing low, within fifty feet of the grasstops, was a marsh hawk, on the hunt for food for her nestful of young. The bird's keen eyes swept the marsh, alert for the least sign of movement below. As she soared above the stream, the hawk saw the king snake wriggling along the surface at full length, helpless. She folded her wings and dived, as swiftly as a falling stone. The hawk splashed into the stream with huge curved talons extended, beating her broad wings amid silvery spray. She rose, holding the king snake in one sharp claw, her talons tearing its flesh. The bird rose awkwardly, off-balance, grasping the snake in the middle of its muscular body.

The king snake writhed and wrapped itself about the hawk's leg and struck at the feathery breast, again and again.

The hawk veered lower, turned to snap her beak at the snake, reached for the flailing body with her other claw—and then, borne by the tightening coils about her leg, flopped into the marsh grass. The coils of the snake fell away. Hissing, glaring with fierce yellow eyes, and beating her powerful wings, the hawk plunged after the king snake, but it was too late. He slithered beneath the marsh grass and slipped from sight. The hawk flapped into the air and disappeared across the distant marsh.

33

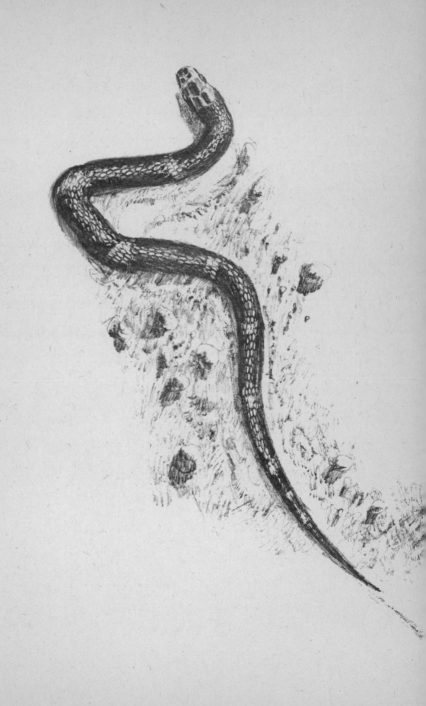

The king snake lay motionless for a time, bleeding from many small wounds, and then crawled slowly and painfully toward his burrow. He halted frequently and left a crooked trail. He no longer moved with a smooth, easy looping of his body; he now dragged his tail behind. For many days the snake lay hidden as his wounds healed, and then, late in his second summer, he emerged to hunt once more. He seemed to move as swiftly as ever, but the powerful back was slightly crooked.

By now the snake was more than two and a half feet long. After he had shed his skin for that season, he lost the scars left by the hawk's talons and seemed to grow faster than ever. He hunted in the late summer woods and along the stream flowing past his meadow, and once more, in the cold days of autumn, he found a hiding place and nestled down deep in the earth to sleep away the winter.

At the end of the third summer only half of the young snake's brothers and sisters were still alive. Many had been eaten by other creatures of the woods, fields, and streams, other snakes, hawks, owls, and herons. One had been killed by a man who mistakenly believed that all snakes were dangerous. Only three or four of the dozen young king snakes hatched three years before would live another year, when they would be fully grown.

At the beginning of his fourth summer the largest of the king snakes was almost as large as he would ever be, more than five feet long, his lean body heavy with muscles. He had now lived about half as long as most king snakes live. He was as strong and swift as any king snake in the woods. He caught his prey easily and skillfully, for he could creep through the grass with hardly a sound and strike before small animals could leap away. Other snakes who came into the small area where he lived were driven away, and no other snakes dared come into his territory at the edge of the woods or into his meadow—until one scorching hot summer day there was little water, and the small stream had died away to a trickle.

On that day there was a loud rustle in the dry grasses beside the stream, and the grasses waved

in the still air. A huge rattlesnake crawled through the meadow, looking for water.

The king snake heard the rustling as he moved through the meadow. He lifted his head high, arching his body in the air, until he was almost halfway off the ground. His long black forked tongue picked up the scent of an enemy. He moved forward and saw the thick body of the six-foot rattlesnake. The rattler was much larger than the king snake. In his upper jaw were long, hollow, curved fangs, used to inject poison into the bodies of his prey.

But king snakes could not be killed by this poison. They alone among snakes are immune to the bites of rattlers, moccasins, copperheads, and coral snakes, the only poisonous snakes in North America. It is because they often kill deadly snakes that king snakes were given their name.

The rattler heard the king snake crawling toward him. Quickly he coiled his great body and shook the rattles at the tip of his tail: *R-r-r-r-r-r!* The sharp, dry, whirring sound could be heard far across the meadow. The rattler's pointed head turned, and his tongue flickered as he looked about for an enemy.

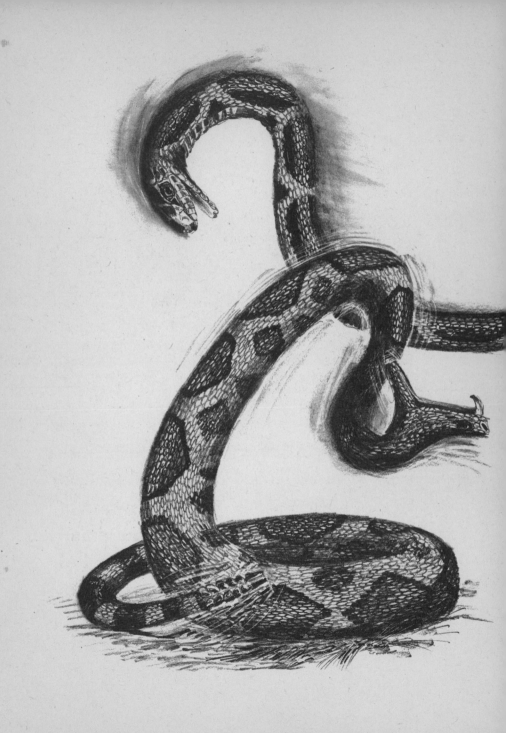

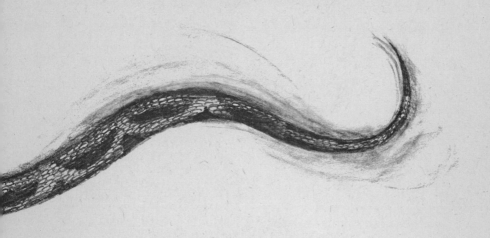

Then the rattler smelled the king snake and uncoiled, for he could not fight this enemy with his fangs alone. The rattler now held his head low to the ground and raised the thickest part of his body in the air. The king snake threw himself at the rattler but was struck by the raised middle of the rattler's body and knocked far to the side.

The king snake whirled and wrapped himself about the rattler, but was not quick enough to escape the stroke of the fangs. The rattler tore the black and yellow scales and left a bleeding wound. Still the king snake hung on. He wrapped himself more and more tightly about the rattler, with muscles bulging along his back. He writhed until he had coiled himself around the heavy body from head to tail. Then he squeezed even harder. The rattler could no longer strike. He could not straighten his body.

The two powerful snakes struggled in the grass, twisting and flailing. Over and over the rattler shook himself and tried to turn his body, but he could not free himself from the black and yellow coils. The snakes tumbled to the bank of the dry stream and then into the slow trickle of water on the sandy bottom. They flung sand and water into the air as they fought. For a long time the rattler tried to break the grip of the king snake, but the strong muscles in the dark body held tightly.

The king snake seemed to squeeze harder and harder, the more wildly the rattler flung himself about, until at last the huge body turned more slowly. The rattler grew weaker and then lay still for a moment. He burst suddenly against the strangling coils and struggled on, but soon the big body grew limp and was still. The king snake hung on for many minutes longer and then uncoiled. The rattler was dead.

The king snake crawled slowly to his old log in the woods and lay quietly until the next morning. He felt weak and tired. But his wounds soon healed, and he returned to the meadow to hunt for food.

When he came out of his burrow the next spring, the king snake did not stay in his meadow. He swam the stream and crawled through a field into woods where he had not been before. He caught a mouse and a few insects but found no other food in the place. Still, he moved about there for several days.

One morning in April he saw another snake sunning on a rock. He crawled closer, flickering his tongue. The stranger was a female king snake, about four feet long. She raised her head, waved her tongue in the air, and glided from the rock.

The male king snake slid along beside her, and they crawled slowly through the woods, their bodies touching now and then. The female then lay still, and the big king snake rubbed his chin over her, moving his head up and down her body. Soon he wound his tail about the female, and the two bodies wriggled slowly. This was the courtship of the king snakes.

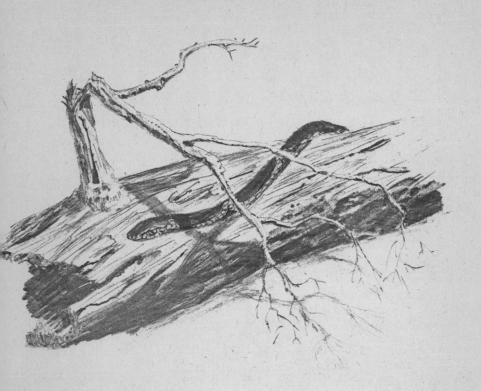

As the two snakes lay close together, another male king snake suddenly crawled over a log toward them. He was almost as large as the big male. The larger snakes rushed together. The female coiled to watch.

The males rose in the air as they met, coiling their bodies and swaying in a sort of dance. They moved apart slowly and came together once more, their bodies meeting and crossing in the combat dance of male snakes in mating season.

The dance grew swifter as the males became excited. Their heads darted through the air as they pretended to strike, but then, as if on signal, both fell heavily to the ground.

The two bodies twined together, and both males squeezed with all their might. The big male forced the other to the ground beneath him until at last the smaller snake loosed his grip, unwound his coils, and hurried away. The big king snake chased him from sight.

The female watched them go, but she did not move from her place until the big male returned.

Now the male and female came together again, side by side. They lay for an hour or more, until they had mated and the male had fertilized tiny eggs carried by the female inside her body through the mating season. Soon the eggs would begin to grow within the female.

The male snake turned away from his mate. He crawled back toward his stream and swam across it, back into his hunting ground. The female did not follow him. She went back to her burrow near the large rock, for king snakes, like most other snakes, do not remain together as mates, but live alone and hunt alone, so that each can find enough food.

More than two months passed, with the body of the female growing heavier. One day she crawled into a hollow log and coiled and turned about until she had made room for a small nest. Then, deep within the soft bits of rotten log, she

laid twenty small white eggs, each about an inch
long. She crawled away and did not return.

On a sunny morning about eight weeks later one of the eggs stirred a bit and a small tooth broke through its shell. Then another egg moved, and another and another, as the baby snakes began to struggle free of their shells.

There was a sudden noise, a rattling of dry grass stalks, and the young snakes became still. Young as they were, some instinct warned them of danger, and they lay quietly as a great black and yellow body crawled past, a few feet away. They were just in time, for in another instant the

big king snake would have seen them and swallowed them one by one as he would any other prey. The young did not move until the huge king snake had gone, a gleaming giant that dragged its tail crookedly behind.

Someday a few of them would be grown up, ready to take the places of their mother and father and other king snakes who had lived before them, in the woods and fields where so many other creatures passed their lives.

About the Author

BURKE DAVIS lives in Williamsburg, Virginia, where he is on the staff of the Colonial Williamsburg Foundation. He has written more than twenty-five books, some for young people, and has written about the Civil War and the American Revolution. He has turned to writing nature books for children and recently wrote *Biography of a Leaf* for Putnam's. He was trained as a botanist and forester and once wanted to become a herpetologist—a specialist in the study of snakes. When he is not writing or working at the foundation, he raises an organic garden above Queens Creek and observes the many animals that live near his woodland home.

About the Artist

ALBERT MICHINI is an illustrator of children's books, a painter, and a teacher. He has taught at the Hussian School of Arts and the Famous Artists School (Connecticut), and at present he teaches at the Norwalk Jewish Community Center in Connecticut. He has contributed to many magazines, including the *Saturday Evening Post, Jack and Jill,* and *Creepy,* and has illustrated many books for young children. He lives in Rowayaton, Connecticut, with his family.